PATTERNS OF BLOOD

PATTERNS OF BLOOD

Zeynep Inanoğlu

An Imprint of Mouthfeel Press

Patterns of Blood

Copyright © 2024 by Zeynep Inanoğlu

Mouthfeel Press is an indie press publishing works in English and Spanish by new and established poets. We publish poetry, fiction, and non-fiction. Our print books are available through independent bookstores and online booksellers, or at author's readings. CLASH! Chapbook Series is an imprint of Mouthfeel Press.

Cover Art and Design by Cloud Cardona

Contact Information:
Mouthfeelbooks.com
Info.mouthfeelbooks@gmail.com

Print ISBN: 978-1-957840-31-4

Published in the United States, 2024
First Printing in English
$12

Contents

For Neriman

PATTERNS OF BLOOD

Photograph from Ras al-Ayn, Northeastern Syria

My people drop
bombs like inflamed
bellies; bodies of phosphorus
white and hungry
falling upon the earth

to birth war : particles
of death become air, a smell
of fire, the holiness
of the human flesh : melting

smoke rising, holding the sky
like a scream.

A gap in a boy's torso
blossoms, a red cavern
where a breathing chest
used to be.

Baby with her leg missing
her black hair curled
and knotted by blood.

How quickly
we made mothers
childless, and
children limbless.

How easily we wielded
our red crescent into
a scythe, how easily
we came to love evil,
and grew from ourselves
this sick, deformed thing.

Deux Arabesques

My sister sits at the piano,
her old friend,
fingers gentle with the
white and black bones
of its wooden body

Rectangular keys mirror
the raw spaces she's
carved on her feet,
red and white grooves
splitting her heels like
fish gills, infant skin cells
revealed by a blade

My sister picks at her body
like she's playing a song:
her mind a heavy vessel
floating somewhere far away

She reaches for the pedals
her toes pressing like pink buds
toward the sun, her notes
like arabesques
extending their limbs
as they fall freely
through the air.

Hagar's Pilgrimage

Flush with seed,
my coveted belly rose
and emptied like a spring
I mothered with water, with
the sweetest relief watched our son
a marvelous creature
expand beyond
myself

Ibrahim, in your pupils
I was an animal
stunned by the image
of its own face
I was cattle, my milk
feral with blood,
my pain, a private
wilderness

where you sent my son
and me to die: hollow
desert in which
no seed can rest
and one must heed
the sun's demands,
to wilt, sullen place
where my breasts
became withered hills
and I ran on bleeding
feet, on skin as bleached
as bone

But God
has provided, has
looked upon my face,
held my meek voice
to his ear, as we named
our first son: *Ishmael*.

Burial Prayer

For Hashem Ahmad Alshilleh

From the earth, you were created
A shepherd for the dead,
your hands weighed down
by dirt and sand, you buried
bodies with quiet movements
your voice steady; guiding the faithful
dead waiting to rest.

To the earth, you shall return
Your grave opening
like a mouth, the soft
arms of soil below
ready to cradle you
like a child, with worms
anxious to pinwheel
in your palms, to feast
on the newly sweetened
patch of dirt.

From the earth, you shall rise again
Pure and rippling with life
you were water, carrying
dead leaves; washing
the earth from them
with your hands: lines of remembrance
on your fingertips, on those
you cleansed, prayed for, buried,
blessed.

Ode to the Working Muscle

My muscle contracts
and its filaments
slide past one another
like fish in a pond

I am expanding

Beneath the skin,
microscopic weavers
restitch the tiny injuries
I have made, my body
taking big,
quick gasps

of oxygen,
the chemical arrangement
of air now
submerged
like a diver
into my blood

I am expanding

My arms broad, strong
they can hold us
both now, can pulse, can
defy gravity like a dancer

I am expanding

A blissful serenade
my working limb singing
to itself, quieting the violent
whispers of thought, enjoying
the throbbing, the inner drum

I am expansive

How excited I have made
each skeletal striation
in my anatomy, and
how imperfectly I have grown
into this newfound heaviness.

The Rhythm (of my love)

The rhythm
by which I love you
is broken
lay your ear anywhere
and you will hear
the difference

The songbird
in my chest
so quiet now
her chirps weary
and relenting

How tired
I have become
by my attempts
to warm you
to pull you
from that dark place
where men go
to sleep
like infants.

Notes on My Father (one)

My father was born
with a nest
of happy
tendrils
on his head
Ringlets
that wave
to each
other
like friends
meeting
for tea

Even in black
and white
photographs
I can see
his locks
as dark
as sea urchin
spines
and his lashes
long
curled
and curious
like a cow's

He is
my grandmother's
last son,
and she
named
him

Hakan
like
Khagan
meaning ruler
meaning *Emperor*

But I pretend
his name means
butterfly:
like the Purple
Emperor
of
the
Nymphalidae
family

that gently
feasts
on honeydew
and tree
sap and
lives happily
by the day,
and then
the month.

Like Daddy, Like Daughter

When you were a boy
the sisters of Istanbul
used to peer
into your stroller
with delight,
gleeful to indulge
in the sweetness
of your baby pink
smiles

Your body a little
cocoon, nestled
beneath blankets
your mother and
her many sisters
knit, bits of wool
fringe hanging
loose and wet from
your wondering
mouth

Ne muhteşem
gözlerin var
bebeğim!

Sang the sisters,
meddlesome
and reverberant,
their compliments
frightened you,
you had been found,
intimately seen
It scared you
and it scares me too

I imagine little-you
as being a lot

like little-me
babbling,
and befuddling
things like *aç*
and *ağaç*
Baby for hungry
or just dreaming
of trees

Little you, little me
both of us
ducklings, whistling
excitedly into earth's ear
Me with your hazel-hued
wings and grandma's
rosy-brown bill

My feathers, finding
home in yours,
and with hesitant
rustles and flutters
embarking upon
the world.

It's Much Too Loud These Days

I need a godly hand
to brush the hair
from my face
and fragment
the rowdy sounds
of the world, the throb
and pound of people
and their voices

to help me eat
when my stomach
feels inverted
and my body
has become tired
of the work
of the constant
upkeep, the being

battered and flooded
by noise
I don't want
to but things
just fall
from me now

and yet I won't
speak, can't talk with
my throat so dry, so torn
I'd rather be a whisker,
the blind bristle
of an animal, silently
gliding its body
through the dark

in search of happiness
So quiet: a mouse
between its paws.

Evening Tics

I grind Tylenol between my teeth
and wait for my liver to explode.
I'm sticky, red drool
running between my legs
and a lunar ache in my belly
I bend in half, try to bring
heat to my body, I look

at my hands, nubbed with
scabs, my nails little pools
of chipped polish, acrylic
islands I've painted and peeled
My mamma used to say
I had a princess's hands
my skin like olive silk
When I'm bad I run
a bath, teach myself how
to swim in womb-like shallows
again. I can mamma too.
I'll be a loom, babies will
leave me evenly stitched
I won't make disorder again.

Refrigerator Note

I'm going to the store
on my list: baby shower cards
and worm food. I'm going
to the store to buy lipstick,
and crushed eyeshadow palettes
want to paint myself
with ugly colors. Want
broken things to feel wanted.

I'm going to the store, alone,
to shop for bleach and box dye.
Need to terminate the black bugs
on my body. Want to
look like Barbie, feel
like Britney.

With me I've got
my lucky number three,
and a dead bee I found
on the walk. Her stinger
wasn't missing. That scares me.

I left the car behind.
Please kiss the dog
and feed the fish.
Don't wait on me.

Afternoon Walk in the Woods

Nature glides her hands
across my tired face
and I turn red and wet
My lashes releasing
black dribble, darkening
the circles below my eyes

Her rain cries for me
when I am weak,
and my rainboots
are quiet and holey

I thank her mud
In it, I am a newborn,
a blade of grass
just a few days old,
upturned and pulsing

I promise her I will sing —
when the birds need a breath,
and nibble on the trees
when the bugs are sleeping

I am her child here,
opening my fish-mouth
waiting for water.

Shirley

In documentaries, reruns
of courtroom footage and case archives

some have heard your screams
that excruciating string of red and black cries

The human ear resists, hears such pain as impossible
cannot admit to the unfurling nightmare

of your death, forty-two years ago
when you were sixteen

and those men raped you, killed you

Left your body, naked and mutilated
in an ivy bush

Shirley: sister and daughter, child and girl
brutalized and beat, begged and bled

There is no moral here.

Letter to My Unborn Child

My alien seedling,
like all young animals

you will come big-eyed
and wailing for milk,
with the smell of softness
and infant-ache
on your breath

But will my planet
be ripe and living enough
to break off another piece
of itself
so that you, little one,
may grow?

With plastic
in your mouth
and mercury
on your tongue

I know
it is not fair of me
to ask you to bear
this struggle

How can I ask you
to leave your cosmic
unknown
for mine?

To live

is to be afraid,
and I am afraid
that you will hurt

because I hurt, and
because my mother
hurt too

My child, you may
never be born
because I,
your mamma,
can't decide
about this earth

Yet I am thinking of you
so often now, my baby,
you are already becoming
in me.

Dancers of Juba

For Robert Battle

By the fist
the dancers of Juba
hold hands, their bodies
hot and blue
like electrical current
These men and women
are sparks of heat,
snippets of fire,
leaping from the sun

Their energy
stout and eruptive
The dancers
of Juba strike the
ground with bare feet
and with their bodies
demand the earth
to quake

Like war
they pound flesh,
bloody, the skin
of their thighs
and ribs like drums
giving beat to their movement

With flexed heels
and bent knees
The dancers of Juba
crack / slice / jump
They bellow without
a sound —

To dance Juba
is to clap oneself
into a thunder

Human storm
fighting itself
black and blue.

Mosquito

In seasons orange-warm,
I swam in the emerald
lake of my lover, resting happily
under his golden awning
until my bliss was broken
by the awful buzz
of a mosquito, gossiping
about my lover, about the sweetness
and rarity of his blood, blood
that I, too, love

In a jealous anger, I spat
at the red-bellied thing
unworthy of pricking
his skin, stealing a taste

but it did no good
she simply sneered at me

O hamae amare
I pity you child
You and your
helpless plea,
Don't you know?
You control nothing!

Creator's Bio

Zeynep İnanoğlu is a Turkish-American poet, pediatric nurse practitioner, and artist originally from Acton, Massachusetts. She has a bachelor's in English Literature from Skidmore College and a Master's from Yale School of Nursing. Her poetry focuses on bodily experience, spirituality, lineage, and medicine. As a writer and healthcare provider, she is especially passionate about the intersection between medicine, art, and the humanities. Her work has been published in *Atlas, Alice Magazine, Folio,* and the Skidmore College's student-run literary magazine. In 2021, she was awarded the Distinguished Writing Award in Poetry by the Skidmore English Department. *Patterns of Blood* is her first poetry chapbook.